Turk Nado

Bruce Martin

DEDICATION

This book is dedicated to
My high school English teachers:

Mr. Norman Foster
&
Mr. Daniel Elmer

~ CONTENTS ~

TURK NADO

The sky is falling!!
The sky is falling!!

-- Chicken Little

1 BETTY'S

It was Thursday and already the third week of November. It seemed to Larry he had just finished setting the clocks back with the end of daylight savings time, but that was two weeks ago, and he still hadn't adjusted to the change. Thanksgiving would be next week, and the news crew was headed out on assignment to some turkey farm in the middle of the state.

Despite the new time difference, it was still dark when the news van loaded up with the crew and equipment. The crew consisted of Jake Newnan (the cameraman and driver), Mel Thompson (the production supervisor) and two reporters – Nora Greene and Larry Robinson.   Their television station was WSPM, the local St. Paul Minneapolis affiliate of a major national broadcasting company.

The van pulled out of the parking garage and turned onto the main road, traveling toward the Interstate. They merged onto the freeway, then headed north on I-494 until it met with the westbound Interstate at the far northwestern corner of the city, and continued a northwesterly heading on I-94 toward the St. Cloud area. Although it was still dark, the crew watched as the surrounding area gradually transformed from a booming metropolitan setting to a rural environment. They passed the truck weigh station and the rest area and then knew they were out in the country. The traffic thinned out and the speed limit increased.

It was about quarter after six when Jake spotted a large bright blue LED sign about two miles up the road.

"Hey, you guys. Do you wanna stop for breakfast?"

This, they knew, meant that Jake was hungry and wanted to stop now. Besides, this was one of the best places to eat along the stretch of highway between Minneapolis and St. Cloud.

"Sure, that's fine," they all agreed.

Jake drove on about a mile, began to slow and turned off on the exit ramp to State Road 101 and U.S. Highway 169. The blue LED sign was now unmistakable – Betty's Truck Stop. Jake slowed down, but still blew through the stop sign at the end of the exit ramp. He pulled into the service area, which was on the opposite side of the road, and stopped at one of the gas islands. The rest of the crew waited in the van while he filled up the tank. Jake got back in the van and then parked it directly in front of the restaurant.

It was still early, and a sign inside the entrance indicated for customers to seat themselves. The restaurant was not yet busy, so they all piled into a corner booth. A few moments later, the waitress came over to the table.

"Coffee?" she asked, as she passed out the menus, and gave each of them a tall clean glass of ice water.

"Yes ma'am," they indicated, and she went off to get the cups and a carafe.

It was often said, if you wanted good food, a truck stop was the place to go. That was no exaggeration, and Betty's was one of the best. By far.

Gina, the waitress, came back with the coffee and poured the cups all around. "Are you ready to order now, or do you need a bit more time to look over the menu?"

They all said they were ready, and Jake ordered first, asking for Betty's Big Breakfast Special – three eggs, three strips of bacon, two sausage patties and hash browns. Then Mel ordered a couple toasted bagels with cream cheese. Nora was trying to watch what she ate before Thanksgiving, so she just wanted a Branberry Muffin with a small bowl of yogurt topped with fruit.

Larry noticed that pasties were on the menu. Since he had not eaten them since moving from Duluth a few years ago, and was feeling a bit adventurous, that is what he ordered -- pasties with gravy.

Once Gina had left for the kitchen to place the order, the others began to chide Jake about his huge breakfast. Jake responded, "A waist is a terrible thing to mind." He meant no harm by his remark, but Larry and Mel felt a bit uncomfortable, especially since Nora was a graduate of Tuskegee Institute, a predominately black southern university. Nora however didn't seem to take any offense, and they went on with the jovial conversation. She apparently knew Jake a lot better than they did.

In a matter of a few minutes, the waitress delivered the orders to the table and then refilled all the coffees. Everything looked, smelled and tasted absolutely delicious. The portions were large, and even Nora's Branberry Muffin (a bran muffin with cranberries) was the size of a small bowling ball.

The conversation turned to the day's assignment.

"So, Mel," Larry asked, "Where exactly are we headed?"

"The Saint Thomas Turkey Ranch. Didn't you get the memo?"

"Yes, of course. I knew that, but just where is it?"

"Oh, it's about twenty miles north of St. Cloud, on U.S. 10," Mel responded. "Just south of Little Falls--about an hour or so from here."

The St. Thomas Turkey Ranch was one of the largest farms in the Minnesota turkey belt, an economic region that stretched across the central part of the state from just west of Elk River to Alexandria. Being one of the largest turkey farms, it was one that had been hit the hardest this past summer. Due to the scorching record temperatures, approximately one tenth of the state's domestic turkey population had died, and the egg production was way down as well. The political angle that was being pushed by the network was of course, the global warming issue. Tens of thousands of turkeys were dying and the farmers would be going broke just before Thanksgiving. The clincher was not global warming, but the fact that turkey prices would be skyrocketing (just like the temperatures) due to diminished supplies. The average family's Thanksgiving dinner would cost fifteen dollars more this year than last.

Hit them in the pocket book. That's how they would get the public's attention.

In actuality, the farmers would see little impact. Sure, they would have fewer turkeys to sell, but the prices for the turkeys would be higher, so most likely it would be a wash. Of course, that would not be part of the news story. Agriculture was a tough business, and the network wanted to play up the plight of the average farmer. The crew had to remember, as the boss had often told them, their job was to boost network ratings, and the news is what sold.

The waitress came back, refreshed the coffees, and asked, "How's everything tastin' to ya so far?"

Everyone told her the food was great. Jake asked for some more bacon and hash browns.

Shortly afterwards, Gina returned with the rest of Jake's food and dropped off the check.

They thanked her for the good food and the great service, and then went back to their discussion. The conversation practically wrote the entire content of the news copy. The point of going to the turkey ranch pretty much would be just to get some live shots and recordings of the birds, and to interview the workers and management of the farm. Of course, the whole story would be carefully edited to fit the political agenda. The public would pay attention to the images and sounds of the turkey farm, and of course to the impacts on their holiday budgets.

Larry happened to remember that as a grade school student he had excelled in show and tell, and now he had found his niche as a TV newsman.

The conversation at last turned to the weather. The summer had been extremely hot, and the days had still not cooled off much so far this fall. The daytime temperatures seemed to be fluctuating quite a bit, with periods of cold followed by a few days of hot weather with highs in the upper seventies. Then the days would get cooler again, but still much warmer than usual for this time of year. It was hoped this pattern would end soon, as it was forecast a strong front would be coming in today, and the temperatures would be plunging toward the low twenties overnight.

The news crew was at last ready to get back on the road. They agreed that the food and the service were both excellent, and so they left a generous tip. Making sure to gather up all their belongings, the crew went to the front door and waited as Mel paid the tab using his corporate credit card. Then they exited the restaurant, loaded into the van and started out again westbound on I-94.

The sky was just beginning to lighten. The air seemed heavy and unsettled, and the dawn gave the eastern sky an eerie red glow.

2 THE FARM

Jake drove along in silence for about twenty minutes while the rest of the crew attempted or pretended to sleep. He finally turned the radio on and tuned to an oldies station that played songs from the seventies and eighties. Billy Preston was singing his hit from 1971:

> *Will it go round in circles?*
> *Will it fly high like a bird up in the sky?*
> *Will it go round in circles?*
> *Will it fly high like a ...*

Jake switched to a couple other stations and found one that was giving the news, weather and traffic. The meteorologist's predictions were for a high today of almost seventy-five degrees by eleven o'clock, with heavy storms coming into the area shortly after noon. There was a threat of severe weather due to the front from the southwest meeting up with a polar vortex that was dropping down from Canada. It would then turn much colder with a chance of snow and overnight lows plunging into the upper teens.

Jake didn't need a meteorologist to tell him that the weather would turn funky. All he had to do was look at the sky and he could tell something was going to happen. The sun was now barely visible, peeking out only occasionally from the clouded sky. Far to the west, it still seemed dark, due either to the early hour, or heavy cloud cover. Perhaps both.

"Hey guys," he announced, "The weatherman says it's gonna snow!"

That got the attention of the rest of the crew, and they began to stir in their seats and look about. The van continued down the highway with the fields now fully visible in the daylight. Most of the farmland appeared to lie fallow. The crops of peas, corn and soybeans had been harvested weeks ago, and many fields were now plowed under, waiting silently in anticipation for next year's planting season.

The sky to the west seemed to be getting darker, as the clouds were starting to roll in ahead of the approaching cold front. A few more miles and the crew began spotting signs for St. Cloud. Several minutes later, Jake turned off on the exit to State Road 15. He passed an unmarked patrol car parked at the side of the ramp, and purposely came to a full complete stop before turning onto the state highway. He then headed north, and after navigating through St. Cloud, continued on 15 to Sauk Rapids. From there, the van merged left on U.S. Highway 10 and continued in a northerly direction toward Little Falls.

They traveled on about eighteen miles before a large billboard came into view, announcing that the St. Thomas Turkey Ranch was only two more miles up the road on the left. Visitors were welcome, and there was plenty of free parking.

Jake maneuvered the van through the entrance to the turkey ranch, and into the guest parking area. Getting out of the vehicle, the crew was almost as excited as a group of kids going on a field trip, not because they would be visiting a turkey farm, but because they were finally at their destination. They were busy unloading the equipment when Mr. Aaron Cole, the owner and general manager of ranch operations, met them.

Mr. Cole had of course been anticipating the crew's arrival. "Welcome to the St. Thomas Turkey Ranch," he exclaimed in his enthusiastic manner. He offered to show the news crew around the ranch, answer any questions they may have, and provide them with plenty of opportunities to get film footage and photos. He would introduce the crew to ranch employees, and they could even meet with the employee of the month if they wanted to. Mr. Cole offered to make himself and the employees available for any interviews the reporters wished to conduct. If there was anything anyone wanted to know about the turkey ranch, all they had to do was ask.

Jake indicated he would want to get some close up footage of the turkeys, and especially some shots of the little turkey chicks--for their cuteness and for the sympathy effect. Mr. Cole was more than happy to accommodate Jake's request, and would make arrangements for him to get whatever photos he needed.

The smell of the ranch was not too overpowering, although the crew could definitely tell they were on a turkey farm. At one point, Larry remarked to Nora, "It's a good thing they haven't perfected smell-o-vision yet, because turkey farms wouldn't play well on TV."

Nora, known for her quick wit, came back with, "Maybe they could run some kind of blurb saying the following material may smell offensive to some audiences – discretion is advised."

"Yeah," Larry replied, "Or maybe the viewers could just turn down their smeller controls."

At any rate, the group tried to stay outdoors in the fresh air as much as possible.

The news crew then took the tour of the ranch, obtained the necessary photos and film footage, and conducted their interviews with the general manager and some of the employees. Then they were in for a treat, as Mr. Cole had arranged for a little luncheon for the crew, the employee of the month, and some of the office staff. The lunch included a hot turkey sandwich with gravy, mashed potatoes, cranberry sauce and dressing. Soft drinks, coffee and pumpkin pie were also provided. Nora of course abstained from her pumpkin pie, but Jake ate his pie and Nora's piece, too.

Once the lunch was over, the crew would still need to go to one of the barns to get a few more close up photos, a bit more live footage, and some sound recordings of the turkeys. They thanked Mr. Cole for providing the luncheon, and then left the office building for one of the main turkey barns.

On his way crossing the parking lot to the barn, Jake noticed the clouds were turning still darker and were now racing across the sky. One distant cloud appeared particularly menacing. A few moments later a light rain started, and the wind, which up to now had remained calm, began picking up. The crew quickened their pace, and got into the barn before getting too wet.

Jake took his camera and sound equipment and began filming some of the younger birds and chicks that were roaming about the barn floor. "I'll finish up with these shots in a couple minutes," he told Mel. "Then we can get in the van and hightail it back to the cities."

About two minutes later the skies opened up, and cold rain began dumping down in buckets.

3 VORTEX

The deluge went on for almost ten minutes and then abruptly let up. It was still raining, but no longer coming in torrents. The wind was now picking up and began lashing against the sides of the barn. Strong gusts sailed across the tin roof, whistling at the corners, and vibrating the metal against the rafters. The wooden barn creaked and groaned. Golf ball sized hail pelted the roof in a staccato that lasted for half a minute. Then the wind eased up briefly.

Mel and Jake thought they could make it to the van, so everyone hurriedly picked up their things and started heading toward the door. That was when they heard the long-wailing sickening sound of the tornado warning sirens. They immediately stopped in their tracks when Jake hollered, "Everyone stay inside and take cover!" -- Good advice, as the barn was a strong and substantial shelter.

The group waited a few minutes while the sirens wailed. The wind had subsided and they no longer heard the rain being slammed against the roof. It was eerily quiet except for the sirens. Then there was a low loud rumble, like a train approaching in the distance. In his years as a reporter, Larry had interviewed many people who had survived tornados. All of them had told him one thing - the sound was just like a freight train rumbling through.

The sound of the train became louder. The crew took shelter in the corners of the barn, throwing themselves on the floor, covering up with whatever they could find, and holding on for their lives. Larry found a tarp, quickly wrapped himself in it and buried his face in the hay. He locked his arms around one of the barn's large support posts, waited and prayed.

Then the twister hit. With a vengeance. The freight train was on top of them and the sound was deafening. The entire building shook as if it were being torn apart. Larry turned his head and peeked out from under the corner of the tarp, still wrapped tightly around his body. He looked up at the roof, and as in slow motion, saw it simply peel away and disappear into the sky. What he saw next is hard to describe. There appeared to be a giant black tube, wobbling around overhead like part of a giant vacuum cleaner hose. Objects were breaking loose from the barn, and were being sucked upward. The turkeys too were being swept up, spiraling skyward into the giant churning vortex overhead.

It was over in less than a minute. The building stopped shaking and the freight train had moved on. But the sirens were still wailing, and Larry still had his arm-lock around the post. He eventually let go, and crawled out from under the debris. He looked around and saw his companions also coming out from their cobbled-together shelter. Everyone was okay; they just had bumps and scratches. But the roof was gone, the turkeys were gone, and most of the barn was gone.

They got to their feet and straggled out into the open. There had been about twenty structures that housed turkeys on the ranch. Most had been reduced to rubble, or had been completely swept away. The trees on the farm had been stripped of their limbs, or snapped in two. They found the news van twelve feet off the ground, wrapped around the trunk of a massive oak.

Mr. Cole, who had been huddled in the main office with many of the staff, rushed out to the grounds to check if the news crew and all the other employees were safe. Miraculously, no one on the farm had been seriously injured. Everyone had escaped with no more than a few bumps and bruises. Finally the sirens were cut, and their pitched warning gradually diminished. After half an hour of continuous wailing, the ensuing silence was almost ear-splitting. Mr. Cole came back to the news crew. He was obviously upset, and Larry at first thought it was because of the extensive damage to the ranch.

"I am so sorry." Mr. Cole started. "This just had to happen on the very day you were visiting us." Unbelievably, he was apologizing for the storm which everyone knew was not his fault. "I just wanted you to have a wonderful time here today, and now just look what happened. I feel terrible."

Mel assured Mr. Cole that it was alright and that it was not his fault. "No one's been hurt. Besides, we are a news crew and this is a big news story. We're here first hand to cover it. There's nothing you could've done to avoid this. We're really sorry this happened to your ranch."

"I'm not so worried about the ranch," Mr. Cole replied. "It will all be covered by our insurance. I just feel bad this happened today while you were here." Then he added, "As a news crew, it's okay if you take pictures and interview us about the storm."

Jake already had his camera rolling, walking around and taking pictures of the damage. As a matter of fact, he had captured the whole storm on tape, as he hadn't turned off the camera when it first hit. He had video of the whole thing – the roof flying off and the turkeys being sucked away. Nora and Larry quickly transitioned to their roles as news reporters, and began interviewing employees and writing copy.

Jake got a shot of Nora standing in front of the tree with the news van twisted around its trunk in the background. Nora began her report, "What appears to be a strong tornado struck the St. Thomas Turkey Ranch early Thursday afternoon, with heavy damage sustained to the buildings and facilities. The WSPM news crew happened to be on assignment at the ranch when the storm hit. You can see some of the damage. Our news van is now out of commission, wrapped around this tree behind me. Our cameraman was able to obtain live footage of the storm, and we will have those amazing pictures for you later. We've been told that everyone at the ranch has miraculously survived with only minor injuries reported. The big question everyone here is now asking – Where are all the turkeys? There were literally thousands of them on the ranch before the storm, and now only a handful remain. This is Nora Roberts, reporting from the St Thomas Turkey Ranch near Little Falls."

Mel asked Mr. Cole, "Is there any way we can get the news crew back to Minneapolis? We have to get this footage back to the station this afternoon!"

"Of course," Mr. Cole replied. "I'll do whatever I can to help you. I'll try to call and see if any of my associates in Little Falls can take you to St. Cloud. I'll call ahead for a rental van from there to the cities."

He left to make a few quick calls, (luckily his cell phone was working) and returned a few minutes later to assure Mel everything had been arranged.

Police and emergency vehicles were already dispatched in force, directing traffic at key intersections and clearing debris off the highways. In the background, the sirens of police cruisers were audible from the nearby roads.

About fifteen minutes later, Mr. Cole's wife, Amanda, drove up in her Chevy Suburban. "Aaron," she called, "Thank God everyone is okay!" Then she asked, "Have them all get in the truck. I'll take them to Avis in St. Cloud, ASAP."

The crew climbed into the SUV with Mrs. Cole, and after saying goodbye to her husband, she whisked them away to the St. Cloud rental car agency.

As they were leaving the parking area, Jake turned around in the seat and stared out the back window at the news van lodged in the huge oak tree. He remembered that he had left his sunglasses in the cab, above the visor..

4   FALLOUT
St. Cloud

Mrs. Eleanor Harris sat in her living room watching the Atmos Channel. She had gone to the supermarket in St. Cloud that morning, and was now relaxing with a hot cup of tea. This was an episode of "Barometer", one of her favorite daytime TV shows, and today they were focusing on strange weather phenomena. Following a commercial break, the first segment covered a fish fall in Yarmouth, England in August of 2000. There were several interviews of the townsfolk who recalled how hundreds of fish had suddenly poured out of the sky, landing in the streets and on their houses. Of course, they were completely baffled as to how this actually happened, but the programming went on to suggest in rare occasions, weather conditions, such as small tornados or violent storms, lift fish from bodies of water and deposit them on land. The following segment was similar, only this time it was about thousands of frogs that in 1973 fell from the sky over Leicester, Massachusetts. Several persons were on film recounting their experiences with the amphibians, or relating how they, as children, had captured and played with the frogs.

Eleanor had just finished her tea when the television picture started breaking up and freezing. She had switched from cable just a few weeks ago, and was already getting bad reception. She heard two dull thuds coming from her backyard and went to the back door to investigate. Two large turkeys lay lifeless in the middle of her yard, and before she could turn to get her jacket, a third hit the ground. She decided to stay in the house. Should she call 911? No, that would be silly, as this was not an emergency. She would just wait awhile before going outside. Maybe she could take the turkeys to the butcher shop later, or donate them to a homeless shelter if they were still good to eat. She thought to herself, "You just don't see turkeys fall from the sky every day." She decided to call the local TV station. Perhaps she would eventually appear on "Barometer" just like those people in England and Massachusetts.

*****

Eleanor Harris was not the only person in the southeastern corner of St. Cloud who was affected. There were several other sightings of turkeys dropping from the sky onto residential areas, streets and parking lots. The fallout was not yet widespread, as only about fifty or so turkeys fell in the St. Cloud area. Nevertheless, some damage resulted from the birds landing on cars that were either parked or were traveling on the roads.

One turkey hit on the lawn outside Mrs. Elliot's classroom. Mrs. Geraldine Elliot was a third grade teacher at the Hampton Woods Elementary School, situated on Hampton Woods Road, just outside of St. Cloud. Her students were all excited about the upcoming Thanksgiving holiday, and Mrs. Elliot was looking forward to the little feast she held each year for her class. Several of her students were looking out the classroom window just as a gigantic turkey landed solidly and bounced a couple times on the soft grass.

"Look, Mrs. Elliot," they cried with glee, "Our Thanksgiving turkey just landed outside!"

Mrs. Elliot took a quick look out the window, spotting the great bird. "Just one moment, stay right here," she instructed her class. "I'll be right back."

She ran outside, hefted up the huge turkey, and ran back to the schoolroom. She proudly displayed it and announced, "Looks like we'll be eating this big fellow next week for our dinner."

The children roared with delight.

*****

Bernie Rawlings had just started his first job on Monday. He was a now a proud new employee of a major discount store on the outskirts of St. Cloud, and his duties included keeping the restrooms clean and collecting the shopping carts from the parking lot. He had just finished cleaning the restrooms, so now it was time to go get the carts. After thoroughly washing his hands, he put on his bright blue and yellow safety vest, and stepped outside. He would try to finish up with the carts as quickly as possible to get back inside the store, as there was a light slow rain. He was in luck, as only twenty or so shopping carts were in the lot. He finished his task in near record time, rounding up all the carts from their corrals, tracking down a few strays and herding them all back inside. Then he spotted one last shopping cart that had just been led out to pasture by one of the customers. He went back out to wrangle the last cart, and was returning to the store. Without warning, one huge turkey plunged directly into the basket. It was as if a water balloon filled with blood and feathers had exploded directly in front of him. In disgust, he wiped the mess from his face and vest using a clean towel he had brought along. He then took one more step toward the store still wheeling the basket, when a second turkey plummeted into the cart. He hastily toweled himself off again, and rushed into the store.

Bernie's supervisor, Ray Foltz, immediately ordered a maintenance worker to dispose of the ruined shopping basket, and personally escorted Bernie to an employee washroom. He helped Bernie get cleaned up and offered him a complete new change of clothing from the store's stock at no charge. Ray double checked, making sure Bernie was okay, and asked him if he needed to take the rest of the day off.

"No thanks," Bernie replied. "I'm okay now, and since there's only a couple hours left on my shift, I'll stay until it's time to leave. But I really don't want to go out to the parking lot for a while."

"I totally understand." Then Ray offered, "Maybe you need to take a good long break."

"Yes, sir," Bernie agreed, "I think I will."

*****

Shayner's Meat Market was having a huge pre-Thanksgiving sale on turkeys. Shayner's was located in a strip mall approximately one mile down the road from where Bernie Rawlings worked. Large wide sections of white butcher paper had been taped to the front windows of the store, announcing this week's special: "Fresh Turkeys on Sale Now." And in smaller letters: "Only $ 2.25 per pound."

At the back of the store, Sam Shayner stood smiling behind his meat counter. He had just sold a twenty-one pounder to Mrs. Eileen Schwartz, and was thanking her for being such a good and loyal customer.

"Mrs. Schwartz, we thank you for your patronage. It's always our pleasure to serve you."

"Thank you," Mrs. Schwartz replied. "You know I would never go anywhere else. Have a wonderful day, Mr. Shayner."

There was a loud thud or crash that came from the roof. Sam went to the front of the store and looked outside as Mrs. Schwartz remained at the counter. Peering out the store window toward the parking lot, he saw only a light rain falling. Everything out front appeared to be normal. Then a small turkey landed on the sidewalk right in front of the store, exploding on impact. Blood splattered against the storefront window, and the crushed carcass lay on the cement in a heap of feathers. Sam immediately went to the back of the store to get a small shovel and broom to dispose of the mess, as he did not want the dead turkey lying on the sidewalk. Certainly not in front of his store! Eileen stayed indoors, and watched as Sam hurried outside with the shovel and a roll of paper towels.

Mr. Shayner was outside for only a minute, but it would be his last. He was crushed by an enormous gobbler that came plummeting out of the air. Sam collapsed on the sidewalk beside the dead birds, while Mrs. Schwartz watched in disbelief. Horrified, she picked up the phone by the cash register and dialed 911.

"Nine-one-one. Can I help you?" said the voice on the line.

"Yes, please hurry," cried Mrs. Schwartz, "I'm at Shayner's Meat Market, and something horrible has just happened. I think Mr. Shayner is dead. Please send an ambulance right away."

"Of course. We'll have an ambulance out there as soon as possible. Can you verify the address for me?"

Mrs. Schwartz found a business card and read the address to the 911 operator.

"We'll have someone there in just a few minutes," the voice promised. And then out of habit, "Have a nice day."

Eileen was still in shock, but hung up the phone and waited in the store. Ten minutes later, the ambulance arrived. The paramedics took Mr. Shayner's pulse and blood pressure, and then confirmed that he was in fact deceased.

Mrs. .Schwartz did not know what to do, as the store was unlocked and she of course did not want to stay there all afternoon. The police arrived and tried to put her at ease. They would secure the store, so she did not have to worry about that. (Eileen showed the deputy the receipt for her turkey, as she did not want to be accused of stealing.) After a very brief interview, the officer told her she could go home if she wanted.

The ambulance then drove off with Mr. Shayner.

Eileen Schwartz drove home with her turkey.

5 HOLIDAY PREPARATIONS
Elk River

Her parents and in-laws would be visiting next week, and Mary Wellbourne was busy preparing her home for the holidays. Her parents would be over only for Thanksgiving, but her husband's folks would be flying in from California and would be staying for most of the following week. She definitely wanted to please her in-laws, so everything had to be just perfect.

Normally, she would begin decorating the house for Christmas the weekend following Thanksgiving, but with the guests, that would be impossible. So she was getting a head start this season, at least with the indoor decorations. The Christmas tree would have to wait until the in-laws left for California, but she could still get pictures, wreaths, stockings and that kind of item taken care of ahead of time. Besides, the kids would be out of school for a few days, and would be excited about the Christmas decorations.

She had to get the house in tip-top shape by Wednesday when Mike and Irma would arrive, so she had a lot to do before then. She would have to go to the cities to pick them up at the airport, so that basically ruled out Wednesday for getting any kind of housework or preliminary baking done. The kids were still in school this week, so she wanted to finish her preparations before next week's crunch.

The rooms were already dusted and vacuumed earlier today. She had finished cleaning the kitchen and the family and dining rooms, and now she was ready to start decorating. Bill had gotten the bins of decorations down from the attic this weekend, and temporarily stored them in the spare bedroom, so at least she did not have to deal with that. After bringing a few of the bins into the family room, she placed a long garland along the mantel. She unloaded the cast iron stocking hangers from their boxes, and also placed them with a few decorative knick-knacks on the mantel. Then she found the stockings, and hung them all in order on their hooks.

All she would have to do next was put up a few pictures over the sofa, and hang the wreath over the fireplace. She decided to take a short break, and went into the kitchen for a snack. The television was on in the family room, but she wasn't paying much attention to it. She did however hear something about a tornado that had struck near Little Falls. There was also something about some turkeys around St. Cloud. She didn't catch it all, as she was busy with the microwave.

While still in the kitchen, she decided to check on her shopping list. Would one large turkey be enough? Or maybe she should get two smaller ones. Let's see … six adults and two small kids … She would get one large turkey. She checked to make sure everything she would need was on her list – ingredients for the pumpkin pie, Cool Whip, cornbread and a loaf of bread for the dressing, eggs, butter, onions, ingredients for the green bean casserole, potatoes, cranberry sauce, and pickles and olives. She would also need a roasting pan, and an assortment of soft drinks. Oh yes – she would need some dinner rolls, frozen vegetables and extra milk.

After finishing her snack, she returned to the family room, hung a few pictures above the couch, and then went to the spare bedroom for the wreath over the mantel. She would need the small step ladder to reach over the fireplace. Once the Christmas wreath was positioned, she stepped back to make sure it was straight. Good enough. She put the step ladder away, and came back to the family room. A few scraps of paper were on the carpet, so she picked them up and then looked about inspecting and admiring the décor.

She was standing before the fireplace when a small turkey sailed out of the sky and dropped down her chimney. On its descent, the turkey bounced off the sides of the chimney flu, dislodging the soot, and then landed with a crash on the fire grate. A cloud of ashes and soot spewed from the firebox, covering Mrs. Wellbourne from head to toe, and settling on a large area of her freshly vacuumed carpet. The disgusting bird lay motionless in her fireplace.

Mary was of course highly upset, and this mishap now set her back at least several hours. She would have to dispose of the dead turkey, clean the room all over again, shower and shampoo, and change her clothes. If the rug was stained, she would have to call a carpet cleaning company. She resigned herself to these additional tasks, and began setting things right.

She carefully picked up the turkey, put it in a plastic garbage bag, and took it to the trash can in the garage.

*****

A few more birds were landing in the Elk River area than had come down around St. Cloud, but the fallout of turkeys was not yet heavy. Nevertheless, the sheriff's department had gotten the word to be on the lookout and people had been advised to stay indoors.

Deputy John Curry was on patrol, traveling in his police cruiser along Main Street when he noticed a woman with a baby stroller standing on the corner at Division. He quickly stepped out of his car, and escorted her to safety, taking her into the Main Street Pharmacy. He explained to the woman, Jenny Foster, that strange as it may seem, turkeys had been reported falling from the sky, and that she should try to remain indoors.

"Where were you planning on going?" he asked.

"We were just going home," Jenny replied. "It's just a few blocks up. Eighth Street."

One of the customers, Carl Estes, overheard the conversation. "I can take you home, Ma'am," he offered.

Jenny said that would be okay, and Officer Curry agreed. So they left and got in Mr. Estes' car, a dark blue Ford Taurus, parked in front of the store.

Officer Curry watched from his patrol car as the Taurus pulled away from the curb and headed up the street. He, too, was about to drive away when a fair-sized turkey hit on the corner sidewalk in the exact spot where Mrs. Foster had been standing with her child not more than five minutes earlier.

"That was a close call," he said to himself, as he picked up the turkey and stuffed it into a nearby waste container.

*****

Grandpa Dillon was at home alone this afternoon, and was getting bored. Usually he would be there with his daughter, Karen, or her husband, Jason Lowery, but Karen had gone out to run some errands, and Jason was at work today. He already had his lunch, as Karen had fixed him a bowl of soup and a sandwich, and had made sure he took his medication before she went out. So he wasn't hungry yet. Besides, if he ate something now, he wouldn't want his dinner, and Karen would be upset with him. He had watched a little TV earlier, but there was nothing he found of interest. He wasn't quite sure what to do. Maybe he would make a pot of coffee. There was no harm in that, and Karen would probably want a cup also when she got home.

He fumbled around in the cupboards, getting out the coffee, the filters, and finding the scoop. The coffee maker was already out – one of those under-the-counter contraptions that also told the time. He filled it up with water, and managed to get the coffee brewing. He was putting the coffee and filters away when he noticed the battery-powered carving knife he had gotten the kids a couple years ago. They would need it next week for the turkey, so maybe he should check it to make sure it was all charged up and still worked. He removed it from its package, inserted the twin foot-long blades, and slapped on the battery pack. He pulled the trigger and the electric knife came alive. He would leave it out on the counter for now.

The coffee maker was still brewing, but it was now making those funny sounds it usually made just before the coffee was done. Grandpa Dillon thought he heard a dull thud outside, but couldn't be sure what it was with the coffee pot still going. He went to the sliding glass door at the back of the house, and looked out. A turkey rolled off the patio roof, and bounced on the lawn. Then another turkey hit the roof and rebounded into the grass. This second bird was slightly larger than the first, and both of them were just lying there. Grandpa went back to the kitchen, grabbed the electric knife and went outdoors. He ventured out into the yard, retrieved both turkeys, and brought them back to the shelter of the patio. He would make quick work of them.

He cranked up the electric knife, and began wielding it, in his mind, much like Darth Vader had brandished his light-saber when he severed Luke Skywalker's lower arm. He quickly lopped off the necks and feet of both birds, as he muttered to himself, "Die young turkey! You have not yet felt the full power of the dark side!"

Only after finishing with the knife, did he realize the extent of the mess he made. The dismembered birds lay in a pool of blood on the cement, their heads and feet scattered about. He would have to wash off the carving knife, clean up the patio, and dispose of the turkeys before his daughter got home. He went to the laundry room and got a bucket of water, some bleach and a scrub brush to clean off the patio. He would also need two plastic trash bags. He placed the turkey necks, heads and feet in one of the bags, and the two carcasses, feathers and all, in the other. After scrubbing down the patio, he put the one trash bag in the garbage can, and the other, containing the two birds, in the freezer. He then put away all the cleaning supplies, carefully washed off the twin blades, and returned the electric carving knife in its packaging to the cupboard.

He poured a cup of coffee, sat back in his recliner, and waited for Karen to come home.

6   THE BURBS
Maple Grove

The Maple Grove Small One-ders Preschool and Learning Center was having the annual Thanksgiving Day re-enactment. The parents were all invited and the children (ages 3 to 7) were dressed as pilgrims, Indians, turkeys, cows, ducks and horses. The Thanksgiving play had just ended, and the teachers and volunteers were about to serve the little feast of turkey sandwiches, potato chips, and apple cider. A light rain was falling, but the festivities were not dampened, as the serving tables had been set up under a large tent in the school courtyard.

Before serving the meal, Mrs. Crofton, one of the first grade teachers, had to gain control of a few rowdy boys. Some Indians were chasing turkeys, and Pilgrims were chasing the Indians. She quickly put a stop to their little game. Restoring permanence of order, however, was not an easy task. The children were all wound up, as they knew they would be dismissed early and would not return to class until the week following Thanksgiving.

Once a semblance of calm was established, the little feast was served. The children ate with their parents and teachers, and then it was time for ice cream and cake. The small cups of vanilla ice cream were brought out along with an abundance of the little flat wooden spoons. Then Ms. Dutton came out with a large sheet cake. The chocolate cake was covered in white buttercream frosting with yellow and brown piping and squiggles around the edges. The top of the cake sported a large frosted turkey with a cartoon bubble caption reading, "Happy Thanksgiving." Ms. Dutton placed the huge cake on one of the long tables. Most of the table was sheltered, but one end extended a foot or so beyond the edge of the tent. The cake, however, was safely at the other end of the table, and would not get wet.

A few minutes later, a large turkey came down striking at the far end of the table. Had it bounced to the left, it would have safely landed in the grass. Instead, it bounced right, rolled across the table and onto the center of the sheet cake. The teachers and parents looked on in shock, as the beautiful cake had been ruined.

The kids didn't seem to care too much, though. They still would have plenty of ice cream, and afterwards they would be going home with their moms and dads. Everyone returned to the classrooms, and once the ice cream was gone, they were all dismissed.

*****

The family and friends of Simon Vincente drove slowly up the narrow lane and parked their cars behind the hearse. They emerged from their vehicles, and walked up the hill, in small groups, to the gravesite. Their black umbrellas collected the drizzle; the rain formed droplets that ran to the edge, hung on for a moment, and then fell as a tear to the ground.

Mr. Vincente had died three days ago from a heart attack while sleeping. According to the obituary, he was born in Cincinnati, Ohio in 1934, and was a member of the First Presbyterian Church of Maple Grove. He had retired as a successful business man twenty years ago, and was survived by his wife Anna, and their two daughters - Brittany Helms of Indianapolis, and Kimberly George of Fort Wayne, Indiana.

The family sat on the reserved bench at the side of the grave, while the others stood in a huddle behind them, umbrellas still raised, while trying to seek the shelter of the green canopy that covered the gravesite. Everyone rose to their feet as the pallbearers labored up the hill, and placed the casket on its supports above the grave. The minister opened with prayer and then recited the twenty-third psalm. He gave a short talk, offered some words of encouragement, and then closed with the benediction. As he was wrapping up the ceremony, a turkey buzzed down, tearing through the canopy, and landed directly on the casket, leaving a small dent in the lid. The bird plopped to one side, slipped off the top edge of the casket, and dropped through a narrow gap into the grave.

Anna immediately fainted, and fell to the ground beside the coffin. Then a second turkey came down, impaling itself on the pointed end of an umbrella. The guests scattered, rushing down the hill to the safety of their cars, while the minister and the daughters worked to revive Mrs. Vincente.

Once she had fully recovered, Anna was escorted to the waiting black Cadillac by her daughters and the minister. They were then chauffeured directly to the funeral home.

That afternoon, the nurses and staff of the Sunny
Acres Senior Living Center were having their
Thanksgiving celebration for the residents. The plans
called for the regular holiday fare of a roast turkey
dinner complete with stuffing, mashed potatoes with
giblet gravy, cranberry sauce, blanched green beans,
and pumpkin pie. A local square dance band had
volunteered to provide the musical entertainment,
following the afternoon meal.

A pavilion was set up outdoors for the band to play,
with hay bales provided for seating, and with autumn
displays of pumpkins and potted mums placed here
and there about the perimeter.

Several of the elderly ladies had visited the center's
beauty salon in preparation for today's special
occasion, and many of the seniors were in western
style shirts and jeans, in keeping with the hoedown
theme.

The residents had just finished their supper, and it
was time for the musical festivities to begin. They
were guided out to the grassy area beside the complex
-- in some cases with their walkers, or perhaps
wheeled out to the pavilion in their chairs. Once
everyone was outside, the band started up with a few

familiar favorites. The lead singer had the seniors join in with several verses of "Old MacDonald Had a Farm" followed by "The Old Oaken Bucket" and "Little Brown Jug." Then the band got into gear with a few other songs and instrumentals – "Foggy Mountain Breakdown" and the theme song from "The Real McCoys." They sang and played all the verses from "The Beverly Hillbillies" and then started up with "Turkey in the Straw." Half way through the song, a few turkeys began falling, punching through the tent and landing in the hay.

The band at once left the tent and disappeared inside the building, leaving their drums and bass fiddle behind. The staff and the nurses managed to get all the residents back safely to the indoor dining room and eventually back to their own apartments.

Later, when asked, the seniors agreed they really enjoyed the party, and that it was the most excitement they had in years. They especially liked the part with the birds.

*****

Robert Boylston pulled his Dodge pickup into the parking lot of Chinella's, a sporting goods megastore located just off of I-94.

He finally had saved up enough to purchase the Browning 12-guage over-and-under that he had his eye on these past eight months. Crossing the parking lot, he glanced upwards, noticing the ominous grey sky. He entered the store and made his way to the gun department. He had already applied for the appropriate permits, so he just needed to pick up and pay for the shotgun. Of course, he would need a couple boxes of shells – regular ordinary target load would do. He bought the shotgun and ammunition at the front register, and went out to his truck. He found the owner's manual in the box the gun was shipped in, and started thumbing through it. WARNING, it read. DO NOT POINT THIS WEAPON AT ANYTHING YOU DO NOT INTEND TO DESTROY. As he was reading the manual, the birds began falling. At first there was just one or two, but within a few minutes, several turkeys had landed in the parking lot.

Boylston loaded up the new shotgun, and then parked his truck right in front of the store. He left the gun in the truck, locked both doors, and rushed to the store's gun department where several customers were milling about.

"There's turkeys fallin' outta the sky!" he exclaimed. "C'mon, boys. Get your guns! Let's have us a real turkey shoot!"

They all rushed outside, grabbed their weapons from the parked vehicles, and started blasting away at the birds as they plummeted toward the ground. The shooting and carnage went on for about fifteen minutes before subsiding.

The deputy sheriff drove up in his patrol car, finally putting an end to their fun. He admonished them sternly and then told them, "I'll let you all off with a warning -- this time."

By then, the guys already had enough excitement for the day. So they packed up all their weaponry and drove off.

7   THE CITIES

Fred Allen was the state's incumbent U.S. Senator, and George Prellar, the current Attorney General of Minnesota, was determined to unseat him. Prellar, a young up-and-coming politician, was mounting a strong campaign, and already had the backing of the Governor, several key members of the State House of Representatives, and the state's Chamber of Commerce. He also had the backing of several large labor unions whose rank and file members had been badly hurt as a result of the country's long-souring economy. The primary elections were six months away, and Prellar was busy crisscrossing the state attending fund raising dinners and political rallies to gain an unshakeable support from the voters and further boost his campaign finances.

This afternoon's rally followed a fund raising luncheon at the downtown Minneapolis Hyatt Regency. There was a lot of speech making at both the luncheon and rally, but Prellar had done all that before. No problem. He was totally up to the challenge.

The five hundred dollar blue plate luncheon included a shrimp cocktail appetizer, grilled lobster and filet mignon, a loaded baked potato, and grilled asparagus. French Silk pie and expresso were served for dessert. Following the luncheon there was a short photo session with the Governor and a few other state representatives, and with some labor leaders who had broken ties with the Allen camp. Of course, there were a few pictures with his family, and also the mandatory shots with babies kissed on the cheek.

Once the luncheon and the photo session were over, Prellar and his close associates were taken by limousine to the rally at an outdoor plaza just a few blocks away. The crowds had already gathered by the time he arrived, and had been whipped into a frenzy, chanting "Prellar, Prellar! He's our Feller!" George stepped out of the limousine, entered the outdoor square and sat down at one end of the stage. The crowd went wild. After the applause finally subsided, the Governor went to the podium to welcome everyone and introduce the state's Attorney General.

"Ladies and gentlemen," he announced, "It is my distinct pleasure and honor to introduce to you the next senator of the great state of Minnesota – the Honorable George Prellar."

The crowd went wild once again, and the band started up, playing the opening bars of "Happy Days are Here Again."

Prellar rose to his feet, but before he could make his way to the podium, a gigantic turkey came down, landing directly in the center of the stage. Blood and feathers flew everywhere. Prellar, the Governor and other dignitaries were quickly escorted to a restaurant immediately off the plaza and then were whisked off to the local party headquarters.

Several more turkeys rained down, dispersing the crowd and the press.

*****

His Lear Jet was parked on the tarmac, and his private pilot was already on board, ready to go, when Nate Kristen arrived at Northern Lights Regional, an airport situated several miles northeast of the cities.

Nate had just negotiated a multi-million dollar contract with NSM – North Star Media, and was eager to get back to Atlanta for the weekend. He had heard the weather forecast, and wanted to get out of the Minneapolis area before the brutal weather hit. Being a native southern boy, his thin blood could not tolerate the wrath of Minnesota's cold weather.

He climbed aboard the small jet, and the stair ramp was raised and locked to its stowed position. Nate securely buckled his seat belt as the pilot revved both engines and taxied toward the runway. His attendant asked if there was anything he would like to drink.

"Yes, the usual," he replied.

She came back with a scotch and soda, and also with a glass of pristine water.

"Here you are, sir. Would there be anything else?"

"No, that will be all for now." Then he added, "Thank you."

After a minute she asked how his meeting had gone.

"Brutal," he answered honestly. "But we got what we came for," and smiled.

"Glad to hear it, sir. I mean, that it was a success."

"I'll just be glad to get back to Atlanta."

"We should be on our way in a few minutes." She then left to prepare for takeoff.

The plane stopped for a moment when it reached the runway. The pilot looked about and checked his instruments. Good. There was no other traffic. Since this was a regional airport, there usually were only a limited number of flights. They obtained clearance from the tower, and he checked one last time. Everything was A-okay.

He revved the engines way up and released the brakes. The plane took off like a shot and in a few moments, was in the air. The pilot raised the landing gear and pulled back on the controls. The plane climbed quickly and the pilot banked left, toward the west, and directly into the wind to gain even further lift. Ahead, he saw the shelf of heavy dark clouds; he continued the rapid ascent and rose above them. Then he spotted another large cloud formation, well overhead. A few moments later, the plane encountered severe turbulence and began shaking violently.

Suddenly the windshield cracked, then shattered. Bird strike! The pilot saw the blood streaming from the edges of the shattered glass panel. Another large white bird hit the windshield, and the plane jerked and shuddered in the air as dozens of turkeys were sucked into the twin jets. The engines sputtered, then clogged and stalled. The plane began descending in a slow gradual dive. The pilot tried desperately to restart the engines, but they were dead. He struggled at the controls, but all he could manage was to steer the plane along its continual, constant descent.

The jet crashed about twelve miles northwest of Minneapolis. It flew into a large stand of trees, broke apart, and burst into flame. No one on board survived.

*****

The WSPM news crew was approaching Minneapolis on eastbound I-94. Jake was enjoying the handling of the black Cadillac Escalade that Amanda Cole had rented in St. Cloud, and busied himself with the radio and navigation controls. He paid only minimal attention to the dozens of turkeys that littered the roadside and fields on the way. At first, there were not that many birds along the road, but as they continued down the interstate, the crew began to spot the lifeless lumps more frequently.

At last, Jake took notice. "Looks like some poultry truck was having a problem losing its load," he remarked.

"I don't think it's a truck dropping the turkeys," Nora observed. "Otherwise they would be only near the road."

The dead birds could be seen lying here and there in the fields. There wasn't an excessive number, but the crew had passed maybe one or two hundred birds along the road so far.

The outside temperature was continuing to drop, and by this time was below freezing. Jake checked the outdoor temperature readout on the Escalade's dashboard – it showed twenty-eight degrees. A heavy snowfall was starting, and wind gusts were blowing the snow across the road in sheets.

They had already passed Elk River and Maple Grove, and were approaching the point where I-494 splits south from the main interstate. Off in the distance, four or five miles to the north, a dense plume of smoke was rising above the tree line.

"It looks like someone crashed and burned," Larry commented. "Do you think it was a gas tanker?"

"Don't know," Jake answered. "We'll find out in a little bit, I guess. Looks pretty big."

Jake turned the radio to the news and weather channel. They were forecasting heavy snow during the rush hour, and consequently traffic would be a nightmare. "This just in," the announcer went on,

"There are reports a private jet crashed just after takeoff from Northern Lights Regional. No word yet on survivors. Prior to the crash the pilot radioed a distress, indicating severe turbulence and engine failure. In other local news ... a tornado was spotted near Little Falls ... And there have been a few isolated reports (and I'm not making this up, folks) of turkeys falling from the sky."

Nora began, "Do you think all that smoke was from the plane crash?"

"Could be," Jake responded.

"What about all those turkeys we've been seeing? Do you think they're from the tornado?" she asked.

"Could be," Jake replied.

During the ride back to Minneapolis, Mel had been in contact with the station over his cell phone, keeping them apprised of what had happened at the farm, and of their progress on the return trip. With the poor weather conditions, the cell phone coverage had been spotty at best. Still, the folks back at the station were aware of the news crew's situation, and were ready to start editing and producing their exclusive story upon arrival.

Jake drove on for a few more miles as the snowstorm gained strength. Judging from the appearance of the clouds, the worst of the weather seemed to be toward the north, and luckily they would be heading south. The road signs signaled the reduction of the speed limit; Jake slowed slightly and then turned off on the southbound 494. The snow, still heavy, began to accumulate on the road. After several more miles the traffic slowed, came to a crawl and stopped. Red and blue lights flashed on the road ahead, indicating an accident. An ambulance and patrol car whizzed by in the emergency lane with their sirens blaring. There was a shallow dip in the road ahead, and Jake could see what looked like an overturned jack-knifed semi at the top of the hill.

The Escalade crawled along the highway, and made its way around the accident. Traffic then picked up slightly, but Jake decided to get off the interstate. He turned off at the next available exit, took some back-way surface roads, and eventually got the crew back to the TV station.

8   NEWS ROOM

When Larry and Nora arrived at the station, they immediately began working with the technical staff to get their report ready for the Ten O'clock News. Jake left to take the SUV back to the local rental agency, and one of his buddies from the station also went off to give him a ride back. In the meantime, Mel went upstairs to meet with the producers and his boss.

Nora and Larry felt their material held two separate stories. The one being the news story they went out to Little Falls for – the report about the St. Thomas Turkey Ranch. The other big story was, of course, the tornado. Nora picked up the phone to discuss her ideas with Mel. She wanted to run the piece on the turkey farm first, even though it was a human interest story, and traditionally human interest stories aired at the end of the news program. Doing the turkey farm first, she pointed out, would be less confusing for the viewers, and it would flow together better in sequence with the second story about the tornado. Besides, the focus of the turkey farm story would be centered on the climate change issue, which was always one of the big news items. The tornado, the second news story, was arguably the direct result of the changing climate. Mel went along with her suggestions.

So they decided to open with the turkey ranch story, and then transition to the piece on the tornado. The technical folks and the weather people were going over some pictures and video that viewers had sent in to the station from their cell phones. Some were just pictures of snow accumulated on picnic tables and cars, but several were of turkeys that were falling out of the sky, or that had landed in peoples' yards and driveways.

The team felt this could be included following the report on the tornado, and just before giving the regular weather report. After the weather segment, they would transition to all the traffic accidents and hazardous travel conditions resulting from the heavy snowfall that started during rush hour. Somewhere in all this they would need to cover the crash of the private jet. Since they couldn't substantiate the crash was weather related, they would make it a standalone story following the weather and traffic segments.

They would go to a commercial break, using the jet crash story as a teaser, and then give the actual report on the jet crash after the commercials. After that would be the sports segment – the upcoming NFL games that weekend, and of course the games that would air Thanksgiving day. Then the food segment, focusing on the perfect Thanksgiving dinner, and lastly, the human interest story on the upcoming holiday shopping season.

Nora called Mel again, and he agreed with all their ideas, offering only a few minor suggestions.

"Okay," Nora summarized for the group, "We'll start with the turkey farm, and then go to the tornado. After the first commercial break, we'll do the weather segment, first with the cell phone footage and pictures of the turkeys, then the regular weather segment. Then we can transition to the impacts of the weather on travel. After the second commercial break, we'll do the jet crash and move on to sports, the food segment, and lastly the piece on holiday shopping."

Everyone agreed with the story lineup, so they all got to work doing their parts editing, writing, and putting the program together. After a couple hours and some fine-tuning, everything was ready for the news anchors, and the weather and sports desks.

Ten o'clock came along, and the news program went off without a hitch.

In the meantime, Jake had returned to the station. "Man, it is really snowing out there!" he exclaimed. "And there's a few turkeys out in the streets."

No one paid particular attention to his last remark, as they thought he was referring to some drunks running around outdoors in the snow.

Even though Nora's and Larry's apartments were within a few blocks of the station, Jake offered to take them home following the broadcast. Both Nora and then Larry accepted his offer, as it was late when they left the station, and the weather was still a mess.

Jake dropped Nora off at her place first.

"See you tomorrow morning," she shouted. "Remember, we don't have any assignments first thing, so we won't need to be back to the station until around ten thirty."

Jake then drove over to Larry's place and dropped him off.

"Thanks, Jake, for the lift."

"Don't mention it," Jake responded. "Have a good evening." Then Jake drove off.

Larry turned and walked up the steps to his building.
He was fumbling for his keys when he heard a dull
muffled thud. A turkey had dropped into the snow
about fifty feet behind him. He hurried with the keys,
entered the lobby of the apartment building, and took
the elevator to the seventh floor.

He entered the apartment and hung up his overcoat.
He went to the fridge, made a sandwich, and grabbed
a cold can of Pabst. He flipped on the TV, started
the DVR, and watched the newscast that had been
recorded.

"We did a darned good job today," he thought. "It's
a good thing nobody got hurt."

They would have to send a note of thanks to Mr. and
Mrs. Cole for their help and hospitality today. He
would get it taken care of in the morning. He should
probably let them know the crew got back safely to
the cities, and also say something about how sorry
they all were about the damage to the ranch.

Larry decided to set his alarm for seven the next
morning. That would give him time to get breakfast,
and then take a walk around the neighborhood before
going to the television studio.

9 AFTERMATH

It was seven, so Larry's alarm clock began playing music. It was an older model clock radio he had picked up at some swap meet a few years ago, but it still worked just as originally designed. After a few minutes of Led Zeppelin, the announcer came on the air. The current temperature was seventeen degrees, and the cities had been hit by a major storm overnight, dumping a foot and a half of snow. High winds and wintery conditions forced officials to close the schools for the day, and only essential state and local government employees were to come to work. Due to treacherous driving conditions, the mayor was advising people to stay at home, if possible.

That wasn't all. Freak weather conditions, coupled with a strong tornado that had hit the turkey farms west of St. Cloud, caused thousands of the birds to be dumped on the city. The passing storm system had left both the snow and the turkeys in its wake. The skies were clear now, but people were warned to avoid direct contact with the dead frozen birds, and especially not to eat them. "If you see a turkey on your property, do not touch it. Pick it up with gloves or a shovel, and place it on the street near the curb. Sanitation and snowplow crews will dispose of the dead turkeys. Again, do not touch and do not eat these birds. If you have any questions, you can call the city's special information hotline at 1-800-TURKEYS. That's 1-800-887-5397."

Larry cleaned up, and got dressed. He gulped down a quick breakfast, consisting of a cup of coffee, a glass of watered-down orange juice, and a breakfast burrito warmed in the microwave. It was not a satisfying meal by Jake Newnan's standards, but it was good enough to start Larry's day. He donned the overcoat, his scarf and a warm winter hat, and left the apartment. He would take a casual walk to look around the neighborhood, and then head over to the station.

Larry took the stairway down to the lobby and went outside. The sky was a clear brilliant blue, and the air was frigid. It was so cold that when he inhaled deeply, his nostrils closed shut and momentarily froze together, and the dry cold air burned at the back of his throat. He started off, taking his normal path

around a few blocks and through the park before
going to the office.

*****

The mayor had already held an urgent conference call
with the city manager, the head of emergency
operations, the police chief, and the park
commissioner. The main point of the call was to get
the city back on its feet--pronto. That meant clearing
the snow, as well as cleaning up and disposing of all
the dead birds. The public needed to be informed,
but not put into a panic. This was totally manageable,
and he expected it to be handled professionally, safely
and quickly. With Thanksgiving coming up next
week and the Vikings playing at home on Sunday, he
wanted the streets cleared within twelve hours. The
first priorities of course would be the major roads,
and the downtown area. Next Friday evening would
be The Holidazzle Parade downtown at the Mall,
kicking off the holiday shopping season, and he
expected the city to be spotless and fully recovered
well before then. His exact words: "Every one of
those blasted turkeys needs to be cleaned up and
properly disposed of."

The heads had received their marching orders, and immediately got the wheels in motion coordinating the cleanup. Within forty minutes, the snowplows and sanitation crews were already hitting the streets.

*****

As Larry went about the neighborhood, he noticed some folks were out with their shovels and snow blowers clearing the sidewalks and driveways. A couple of the neighbors were dutifully disposing of their dead turkeys, picking them up carefully with snow shovels, and depositing them at the curb. One man, however, while clearing his walkway with a snow blower, hit a small lump protruding above the snow. The blower strained and faltered for a moment, then a mix of feathers and blood-red snow flew from its exhaust chute.

By the time Larry had walked a few more blocks and circled back around to one of the major intersections, the snowplows were out in force clearing the main roads. In addition to the snowplows, there were teams of tree surgeons that had been recruited to dispose of the collected turkeys. Larry noticed one truck parked at the side of the street with a tree and brush grinding machine positioned directly behind it.

He watched as the workers started the brush grinder, with its rotary blades gaining momentum, reaching a high pitched whine. The workers then busied themselves with pitchforks, tossing the frozen dead birds into the hopper. The high whining of the free-turning blades would be interrupted for a moment as the turkeys were shredded, and the remains were spewed into the waiting truck. The machine would then regain momentum, as its blades continued to spin.

Larry watched this whole operation in awe, much like a youngster who is fascinated by watching men dig a hole in the ground.

He continued observing the tree surgeons for several minutes. He finally decided to go on to the TV station.

*****

Larry walked the nine blocks to the studio, arriving right about nine fifteen. He was earlier than most of the crew, so he grabbed a cup of coffee and a doughnut, and then went to his office to relax a bit and catch up on e-mails. With the exception of Mel, the rest of the crew made it to the station around twenty minutes after ten. Mel, being their boss, made the big bucks, and usually was one of the first to arrive and last to leave the office. (It was Mel who had made the coffee and brought in the doughnuts that morning.)

The crew was ready, and Mel began their meeting right at ten thirty. Today they would cover the aftermath of the storm. Jake, Nora and Larry would go out to film and report on the cleanup efforts – the snowplows clearing the streets, and the sanitation crews cleaning up the turkeys. The newscast would of course re-run last night's stories about the turkey farm, the tornado, the plane crash and yesterdays' traffic problems; but today the stories would be expanded to include the extreme overnight weather conditions, and the turkeys that had been dropped on the city. They would also continually run the public service announcements regarding collection of the dead birds and the information hotline. The weather desk and traffic center would coordinate their reports to include new footage and reports on any breaking developments on the area's roads and highways.

They were about to wrap up the meeting. "Any questions," Mel asked?

There were none. Everyone knew what was expected.

"Good," Mel pronounced.

They all started work on their presentations and the tasks at hand.

Nora, Larry and Jake started about the city, interviewing snowplow crews, a spokesperson for the Department of Public Safety, and a director for the Department of Parks and Recreation. They obtained captivating footage of the turkey cleanup operations, and some photos of a few minor fender benders around town. To cover the human interest angle, the crew filmed a few groups of kids building snow forts, and having the time of their lives in a huge snowball fight.

After all, school had been cancelled for the day.

10 RESTORATION

Despite the major challenges, by Friday afternoon the city workers were successful in clearing the main streets and roadways of the snow and dead birds. In fact, only a minimal number of outlying residential streets remained to be cleared by nightfall on Saturday. It was indeed a Herculean task, but the turkeys had been removed from the cities' roads and parks.

As a consequence, the Thanksgiving holiday was a huge success, with the Holidazzle parade kicking off the downtown shopping season on schedule Friday evening. The festivities went just as planned, without disruption, and the shoppers could get about freely downtown without any problems.

The scheduled sports venues also went without a hitch. The Vikings defeated the Chicago Bears Sunday afternoon in a nail-biter before a sell-out crowd. The final score was twenty to seventeen, with the Vikings blocking a Bears' last minute field goal attempt. The clock ran out, the game ended, and the celebrations began.

The area had fully recovered from what the weathermen on TV dubbed as "Turk Nado -- the weirdest storm ever to hit the cities."

The many successes were faithfully and meticulously reported by the entire news team of WSPM.

On the personal level, Larry coordinated with Mel and the rest of the coworkers in sending a note of gratitude to Mr. and Mrs. Aaron Cole, thanking them and the people at the ranch for their kindness and hospitality. Sincere wishes were sent for the full and rapid restoration of their ranch in the wake of the severe storm damage.

Several weeks later, Larry received a reply from Mrs. Cole indicating that they had been fully remunerated for their losses, and that all the ruined property was being replaced with new barns or structures. They expected the ranch to be back on its feet and fully operational by the end of March, and the news crew was welcome to come back any time and visit them again.

Regarding personal relationships, Jake and Nora began dating right after Christmas, and within a month or two, things had become quite serious. Jake's demeanor gradually changed, and he began taking off a few pounds. He confided with Larry and Mel he had gone on a diet, and his goal was to lose fifty pounds by August. "I need to look good in a tuxedo," he remarked. The following Monday, Nora came to work with her new engagement ring.

*****

One afternoon in mid-March, several boys had gotten off the school bus and were walking along the residential street leading to their homes. The weather was by then warming up a bit, and the layer of ice that had covered their street during the winter was finally beginning to thaw, breaking into large sections one to two inches thick whenever an occasional car passed by. The boys made a game of stomping or jumping on the ice covering the road until substantial chunks broke off. They would then pick up the flat sections and throw the ice as far as they could – usually about fifteen feet. Under one chunk, they found a frozen intact turkey, flattened out by the winter's automobile traffic. The bird's head and neck, frozen solid and still attached to its body, would function as a perfect handle, so one boy picked it up and gave it a fling. The flattened turkey sailed through the air, beak over tail feathers, much like a large Frisbee. Its trajectory gradually curved, and the bird landed, slicing into a snowbank in a neighbor's front yard. The boys laughed, and nicknamed the flat frozen turkey their "sail-bird."

*****

George Prellar went on to handily win both the primary and general elections. In January of the following year, he would be going off to Washington as Minnesota's new senator; and thanks to sixty-five percent of the electorate, old Fred Allen would be retired, for good. In a last ditch effort to remain in power, Allen had tried to play every dirty political trick in the book, but in the end, all his false accusations and half-truths backfired, and he lost big.

*****

Two other events relating to the storm bear mentioning.

In May, the ATMOS Channel sent a production team to the St. Cloud area to film a series of episodes for their program, "Barometer". The series, a full documentary of the "Turk Nado" weather phenomenon, was closely coordinated with the local news organizations, and especially so with the news team of WSPM. ATMOS used much of the footage captured by Jake Newnan, and many of the photos and videos that viewers had sent in. Persons interviewed by ATMOS included Bernie Rawlings, who offered the details of turkeys crashing down into shopping carts, and of course Eleanor Harris, who was absolutely delighted to be featured on "Barometer".

*****

It was late in October when Grandpa Dillon suffered a severe stroke, was hospitalized and then transferred to a nursing facility. He was there for two weeks until he passed away.

He was on his deathbed, and was largely unresponsive. During the last two weeks, his daughter, Karen, and her husband were continually at his bedside, but that day they were visiting for the last time. Grandpa unexpectedly turned his head toward Karen and opened his eyes.

"Karen," he murmured weakly, "There's something … I need to tell you."

"Yes, Dad? What is it?" Karen asked tearfully.

Before he closed his eyes and went to sleep, he uttered these final words. "I'm sorry … ," he began, "Karen … when you get home … be sure to … check in the freezer."

Turk Nado

&&&&&

Will it go round in circles?
Will it fly high like a bird up in the sky?
Will it go round in circles?
Will it fly high like a bird up in the sky?

-- Billy Preston 1971

ABOUT THE AUTHOR

Bruce Martin is a native of the Detroit Michigan area, and is a 1965 graduate of South Lake High. He holds a Master of Arts degree from Wayne State and a Bachelor's from the University of Michigan. A Vietnam Era veteran, he was enlisted four years in the U.S. Navy, and was stationed aboard the USS Davis, homeported in Newport, Rhode Island. He has since retired from the insurance industry, and resides in Northeast Florida with his wife and two of his three sons.

Bruce's first published work was <u>Crafted Web</u>.

<u>Turk Nado</u> is his second book.